Of Mice and Aliens

More Asperger Adventures

Lisa and the Lacemaker
An Asperger Adventure
Kathy Hoopmann
ISBN 978 1 84310 071 3
eISBN 978 1 84642 354 3

Blue Bottle Mystery
An Asperger Adventure
Kathy Hoopmann
ISBN 978 1 85302 978 3
eISBN 978 1 84642 169 3

By the same author

All Cats Have Asperger Syndrome
Kathy Hoopmann
ISBN 978 1 84310 481 0

Haze
Kathy Hoopmann
ISBN 978 1 84310 072 0
eISBN 978 1 84642 405 2

Of Mice and Aliens

An Asperger Adventure

Kathy Hoopmann

Jessica Kingsley *Publishers*
London and Philadelphia

First published in 2001
by Jessica Kingsley Publishers
73 Collier Street
London N1 9BE, UK
and
400 Market Street, Suite 400
Philadelphia, PA 19106, USA

www.jkp.com

Library of Congress Cataloging in Publication Data
Hoopmann, Kathy, 1963-
    Of mice and aliens : an Asperger sdventure/ Kathy Hoopmann.
        p. cm.
    Summary: Ben's attempt to cope with his newly diagnosed Asperger Syndrome is
complicated by the crash landing in his back yard of an alien who knows nothing   about
Earth'c rules and norms.
    ISBN 1-84310-007-X (pbk.)
    [1. Asperger's syndrome--Fiction. 2. Extraterrestrial beings--Fiction. 3. Science
fiction.] I. Title.
    PZ7.H7704 Of 2001
    [Fic]--dc21

                                                                                20010
38163

British Library Cataloguing in Publication Data
A CIP catalogue record for this book is available from the British Library

ISBN 978 1 84310 007 2
eISBN 978 0 85700 179 5

Printed and Bound in Great Britain by Bell and Bain Ltd, Glasgow.

For Errol,
for everything

As from the house your mother sees
You playing round the garden trees,
So you may see, if you will look
Through the windows of this book,
Another child, far, far away,
And in another garden play.
But do not think you can at all,
By knocking on the window call
That child to hear you. He intent
Is all on his play-business bent.
He does not hear; he will not look,
Nor yet be lured out of this book.

– from *A Child's Garden of Verses*,
Robert Louis Stevenson,
1885

Contents

Contents

Prologue

Deep in the darkness of space there was a movement that did not belong. A streak of light sped towards a small blue green planet. It was moving so fast that telescopes could not track it. It was so small, radar did not reveal it. And as it slipped down through the atmosphere... nobody knew it was there.

Deep in the darkness of space there was a movement that did not belong. A streak of light sped towards a small blue green planet. It was moving so fast that telescopes could not track it. It was so small radar did not reveal it. And as it slipped down through the atmosphere ... nobody knew it was there.

Chapter 1

Dreams

Ben sat up with a start. He'd been dreaming. He looked at the clock. 8.01 a.m. So late. Sue, his stepmother, must have gone to school without him. She said she might, last night when he felt sick. Ben lay back in bed, feeling terrible. His head throbbed and the sun shining through the window hurt his eyes. The dream had seemed so real...of flying through space, trying to escape from...he forgot what. For now he was safe. At home. In bed. Relaxing a little, he snuggled under the blankets.

"Ben? Are you awake?" Ben's dad came in and sat on the edge of the bed. "Sue told me you weren't well last night."

"My head aches," Ben said.

"That's no good," said Dad. "You can't go to school then. Grandma will stay with you."

"OK." Ben liked being with Grandma.

"Sorry I've got to rush, but I'm late for work." Dad reached over and gave Ben a hug goodbye. Dad's green shirt had 'Jack Jones for Jobs' neatly stitched in white on the pocket. Ben breathed in the faint scents of sweat, oil and cut grass that even the washing machine did not take away. He loved those smells.

"Hope you feel better soon. Sue's going to ring at lunch to see how you are," added Dad as he left the room.

Ben lay back thinking of Sue. Ben's real mum died when he was young. He first knew Sue as 'Miss Browning-Lever' when she was his teacher at his school. Then she married Dad and they became a family. It was nice to have her around all the time, and Dad was the happiest Ben had ever known him. Sometimes, when he wasn't thinking, Ben even called Sue 'Mum'.

Grandma soon came in carrying her new laptop computer. "My poor little man," she said, giving Ben a kiss on the cheek. "It's no fun feeling sick, is it?"

"No."

"Should I ring Andy's mum and cancel this afternoon?"

Andy was Ben's best friend and he stayed at Ben's house every Thursday after school and on Saturday mornings while his mother went to work.

"I'll be better then," Ben said. He wanted it to be true. He had fun with Andy.

Grandma held up her laptop. "Are you too sick to give me some help with a problem I have with my computer?"

"No." Ben's eyes lit up. He loved computers. He'd never be too sick to play on one.

"I can't get my emails to come up," Grandma said, opening the case and plugging the cord into the wall. "Your dad set this up for me, but now I can't get it to work."

Ben looked at her in surprise. "It's not connected, Grandma."

"But I just plugged it in."

"It needs the telephone connection," Ben laughed. "Come into the lounge and I'll show you." It took only moments for Ben to set up the computer and Grandma's emails quietly 'dinged' as they came up on the screen.

"I'll never get used to these things," Grandma complained. "My old brain isn't made for new fangled inventions."

"Mine is," Ben said proudly. "Asperger brains are made for computers." Ben had only known that he had Asperger Syndrome for a couple of months, but he was proud of the things he could do. Having Asperger's made it hard to understand what other people think and feel, but bytes and micro-chips were easy for him.

Grandma chuckled, "Well I'm lucky you are here."

"You've got an email, Grandma. From New Science Digest. How come?"

"If you really must know, I'm doing an assignment for university."

"University? But you're too old!"

"I might be old, but I'm not *too* old. It's never too late to learn. My assignment is about the possibility of life on other planets, and your dad helped me email the New Science Digest for some information."

"But there is life on other planets, Grandma. Star Trek visits them all the time."

Grandma looked at Ben to see if he was joking.

"Ben," she said, "Star Trek is a TV show. It's not real."

"I know. I'm not silly, Grandma. It's not real yet. But it's all going to happen one day."

Grandma cleared her throat. "It's still just a TV show. It's quite possible there is no life in space at all. Now, Ben, I've got to work on my assignment and you should go back to bed."

"But Grandma…" started Ben.

"Ben," Grandma interrupted, "I know you can talk about space for hours on end, but I have some work to do and you are supposed to be sick. Thank you for helping me, but now you really must go."

Ben sighed in frustration. But he didn't argue. His head was thumping and he knew Grandma was right. He went to his room and lay down.

He did not see a brilliant flash of white light streak across the morning sky.

He did not watch it disappear into the trees at the bottom of the garden.

He did not know his life was about to change.

Chapter 2

Like Nothing on Earth

When Ben woke up again, he glanced at the clock. 11.24 a.m. He'd been asleep over three hours! In the middle of the day! He *must* be sick. Grandma came in and felt his forehead.

"I heard you stir," she said. "Are you OK?"

"I didn't stir anything," Ben said with a frown.

"I mean, I heard you moving around. How do you feel?"

"Better." It was true. His headache had gone.

"Want some lunch?"

"OK," said Ben.

Ben lazed around the rest of the day, watching TV and playing his favourite computer game, *Zarin and the Brain*. When the doorbell rang that afternoon, Ben raced to answer it and saw Andy through the side window. Andy was the tallest kid in the school and the skinniest. He was even taller than their teacher, Miss Peters. He looked like a friendly stork and was the captain of the basketball team. They had been best friends since preschool days and always managed to have fun when they were together.

The boys ate some chocolate cake, Grandma's speciality, still warm from the oven, then headed outside.

"Let's build a fort in the bush," Andy said as he ran towards the track above the gully. Despite his long arms and legs, he ran smoothly, and he was fast. Ben followed along more slowly. He didn't mind being last. Anyway, he thought, you did things better if you took your time.

The track led to the thicker trees at the bottom of Ben's yard. There, the bush was huge and full of great hiding places. Andy, who lived with his parents in a townhouse, thought Ben's backyard was the best.

As he made his way along the track, Ben felt uneasy, but did not know why. Usually the bush was alive with squawking, chattering birds, and rustling bushes that hid lizards and insects. But today everything was quiet. Too quiet. He glanced around, up in the trees and down in the gully, then stopped. He blinked, then blinked again.

"Andy," he called. "What's round and silver and sits on the ground?"

Andy slowed down. "Is that a joke?" he asked.

"No, I mean it!" yelled Ben. "Look!"

Andy jogged back to his friend. Ben jumped up and down on the spot, pointing into the gully. Through broken trees and branches something very strange lay below them. It was round and made of smooth shiny metal. It had a sharp edge around the outside, which glowed with faint pulses of light.

It was very hard to describe.

It looked like nothing on earth.

It looked like…a spaceship!

Chapter 3

There is *Life* in Outer Space

"**I**t's a flying saucer!" Ben cried. "A real flying saucer! There *is* life in outer space!"

"Unreal!" Andy breathed.

"No, it's real all right," Ben said. "Look, it's damaged." One side of the spaceship was crushed and the lights were broken. A quiet hum came from inside. It seemed to be getting louder.

Andy watched nervously. "It could be dangerous. Perhaps we should tell your grandma."

But Ben wasn't listening. "Come on," he said. "Let's get closer." He edged his way down the gully towards the ship. Andy, watching from above, held his breath.

The humming grew louder and louder. Suddenly part of the wall of the ship moved. A sharp yellow light pierced through a crack and into the gully.

"Run, Ben! Run!" shouted Andy, as he threw himself behind a tree. Ben stepped back, watching the crack as it widened. A ramp slid from the doorway and down to the ground.

"Ben!" Andy called. "Run away!"

A smooth grey leg appeared out of the ship. It was long and thin and appeared to be made of jelly. The four suckers on its feet pressed onto the slide with a firm "splock".

"Ben!" Andy screamed.

Ben flapped his hands. Another leg stepped onto the slide. Splock. Then came another leg and then another. Finally out came a round blobby body with a balloon-shaped head. Two eyes wobbled and jiggled at the end of long grey feelers. The eyes suddenly saw Ben and the feelers hardened and stretched towards him like sticks.

"Hello," said Ben. "Welcome to Earth." In an instant, the creature jumped back into the ship. The ramp slid up into the doorway, and the wall closed. All was quiet again, except for the deep hum.

Ben turned to Andy. "I think we frightened it," he said.

"*We* frightened *it?!*" Andy gulped from above. His legs were shaking and his heart was beating fast. "We've got to get away from here. Now!"

Ben stepped over to the spaceship and knocked on the metal panels. "Mr Alien," he called. "Come out. We won't hurt you."

"What are you doing?" Andy shrieked.

"I'm trying to be friendly."

"Friendly? You're crazy!"

The crack opened again and steamy smoke bubbled out of the doorway as the ramp dropped to the ground. When the smoke cleared, a strange boy stood in front of them. His face was Ben's, but his body and clothes were Andy's.

"You're a Shapeshifter!" Ben shouted, jumping on the spot, hands flapping again. "You can change shape!"

"Hello-zzik. Welcome to Earth." The boy spoke with Ben's voice.

"Wow! You can talk too!"

"You can talk-zzik too," it repeated.

"Where are you from?" Ben asked. "The Amargosa System? Beyond Epsion?"

The boy stared at Ben without answering.

"Those are solar systems in Star Trek, Ben," Andy called from behind his tree. "I don't think he's from them."

Ben took a step towards the boy, who took a clumsy step backwards. "Come with us," said Ben. "Are you hungry? I can get you some chocolate cake if you want."

Andy peered out from behind his tree. "Are you crazy?" he shouted. "This thing is an alien. You can't give it cake. It could be here to wipe out the human race for all we know."

"Don't be silly, Andy," said Ben. "It's just crashed. We have to help it."

"But it's got my body and your head! Your grandma will flip."

Ben tried to imagine Grandma doing a flip and decided she was too old for that. He said to the boy, "Andy's right. You'll have to change again. Can you do that?"

The boy stared back. Nothing happened.

"I don't think he knows what we're saying," said Ben. He reached out and touched the boy's face and shoulder. In a blur of colour, the alien transformed. Now it had Ben's body and Andy's face.

"No," Ben laughed. "Mix everything up so that you don't look like us too much."

The boy stared at him. Ben reached out again, but this time he waved his hand around the boy's face and clothes. Again the boy blurred and then a new kid stood in front of him. Ben's eyes and nose were mixed with Andy's ears and hair. He was shorter than Andy, but taller than Ben and he wore Andy's school uniform.

"Perfect," said Ben, as he led the alien boy to the side of the gully. The boy was a bit wobbly as he tried to use his new legs on the slope.

"Wait!" cried Andy. "Where are you going? Don't you see how dangerous this is? We know nothing about aliens."

"It's OK, he's our friend," said Ben. He turned to the boy and smiled. "Aren't you?"

The boy smiled back.

"See."

"That means nothing," Andy yelled. "Think, Ben. It might be our enemy. We don't have any idea what it can do. It could hurt us!"

"You won't hurt us, will you?" Ben asked the boy.

The boy smiled.

"See. He's harmless."

Andy shook his head. "I hope you're right. But you still can't take it into the house. What are we going to tell your grandma?"

"That's simple. We'll tell her the truth. She's studying about life on other planets and now we can show her a real alien."

"What? No way! You can't do that. She'll think we're mad. No one will believe us. I think we should leave it alone. Here."

But he was too late. Ben and the alien boy scrambled to the top of the gully and walked towards the house.

"That's simple. We'll tell her the truth. She's studying about life on other planets and now we can show her a real alien."

"What? No way! You can't do that. She'll think we're mad. No one will believe us. I think we should leave it alone. Here."

But he was too late. Ben and the alien boy scrambled to the top of the gully and walked towards the house.

Chapter 4
Zeke

Sue was home from school. She sat next to Grandma, cutting up vegetables for dinner.

"Hi kids," she said, as Ben and the alien came through the door, followed by Andy.

"Who's your new friend?"

"Zzik," said the alien.

"Zeke?"

"He's from outer..." Ben began, but Andy cut him off and said, "He's from a long way away. He's new here."

"Oh. That's lovely. And how long have you been in our country, Zeke?"

"That-zzik lovely," repeated Zeke.

Sue looked puzzled.

"He's from outer space, Sue," said Ben.
"His spaceship crashed in the gully. It's down
in the trees. Can he have some chocolate
cake?"

Andy groaned.

"Choklit cake," said Zeke.

"Oh, it's a game," said Sue. "Sounds like
fun. I think we have enough cake left for
brave space adventurers. After that you
might have enough time to fix your
spaceship before Andy's mum turns up." She
placed three slices of cake on a tray and gave
them to Ben.

"Good, let's go," said Andy, as he led Ben
and the alien outside.

Sue and Grandma smiled as the kids left
the room. "That's nice," said Sue. "They seem
to be playing well together. I wonder what
country Zeke comes from? I've never seen
him around here before. Or at the school."

"Me neither," said Grandma. "It's strange though. Ben doesn't usually enjoy those sort of pretend games. He's never played cops and robbers, or cowboys and Indians, or that sort of thing. Maybe Zeke should come around more often."

She put down her knife and leant back in her chair. "You know, Sue, Zeke reminded me of Ben when he was young. He took a long time to start talking, and back then Jack and I didn't know he had Asperger's. He often repeated what we said without understanding anything. I suppose Ben must have felt a bit like Zeke, a kid in a new place and not really knowing what other people were saying."

Sue nodded. They had only known about Ben's Asperger Syndrome for a short time. Before that no one really understood a lot of the things he did. "I wish I'd known Ben back then," Sue said. "When I first taught him in class I couldn't relate to him at all. He was...different. Now I understand him better and I think he's a great kid."

While Grandma and Sue chatted, Ben, Andy and the alien finished off their cake outside. Ben cleaned the crumbs and icing from Zeke's face and hair.

He then turned to Andy. "Hey, I beat Zarin this morning. Level ten. Why don't we show Zeke the computer."

Ben led them back into the house and through to the TV room. Ben turned on the computer, and Zeke sat on the floor in front of the TV watching the afternoon cartoons. While *Zarin and The Brain* was loading, Andy turned to Ben. "This is crazy, Ben," he said quietly. "Here we are, playing computer games in your house with an alien watching TV."

"Yep," said Ben. "Great isn't it."

"Ben, you're not listening to me. He could be dangerous. He could be here to wipe out the world."

"He's okay, Andy. He's funny."

"How come you trust him? Because he smiles? Remember 'stranger danger' that they teach us at school? Aliens are strangers too. Who says he isn't dangerous? We have to be careful."

Ben was confused. Zeke seemed so friendly. The two boys turned to watch the alien on the floor. Zeke still sat in front of the TV, making unusual sounds as he tried to copy the voices of the cartoon characters.

"My mum will be here soon," said Andy. "We've got to do something about him. He can't stay here. We've got to get him back to his ship somehow."

"I know what to do," said Ben suddenly. He ran to his room and returned with his portable black and white TV, checking the batteries. "This should work." He stretched out the aerials, and tuned the TV to the same programme that Zeke was watching. Then he turned off the other TV. "C'mon Zeke," he said as he waved the portable TV in front of him.

"Zzik," said Zeke, getting up. He followed Ben and his TV out of the house.

"Too easy," said Ben. "I think we're getting to know Zeke pretty well."

"We still don't know him that well, Ben. Please don't trust him too much. Promise?"

"OK," said Ben.

Soon Ben and Andy returned to the house without the alien. "I hope the batteries last through the night. I couldn't find a power point in that ship," said Ben.

Chapter 5

Nothing like Celesstis4

The next morning Ben's alarm went off at 6.00 a.m. He had set it for 30 minutes earlier than usual. He jumped out of bed.

Just as he did every school morning, he put on his school uniform, then ate a bowl of cereal, packed his school bag, brushed his teeth and combed his hair. He was in a hurry to check on Zeke. He didn't think to check on Zeke first and do his jobs afterwards. That wouldn't be right. There had to be an order to things. Ben liked routine.

Ben ran across the dewy grass and down into the cool of the trees. Then he remembered Andy's words and slowed to a walk. Perhaps he shouldn't run straight to the spaceship. He'd have to be more careful. Tip-toeing, he peered over the edge of the gully. The spaceship was still there. The ramp was down, but Zeke was nowhere to be seen. Ben crept down into the gully just as Zeke stepped out onto the ramp, still in his school uniform. "Good morning, Ben-zzik," he said.

"Hi Zeke," said Ben forgetting his caution in surprise. "You can talk! How come?"

"I learned your language last night-zzik. I have been finding pictures and sounds on different frequency cycles in the atmosphere of Urssus3."

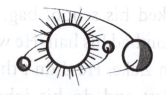

"Wow," said Ben. "What's Urssus3?"

"Do you not know your own planet? Is this not the third planet from Urssus-bul?" asked Zeke, pointing to the sun.

"Oh, we call this Earth and that's the sun. You mean you were listening to the radio and watching TV?"

"Yes-zzik."

"And now you can understand us?"

"Yes-zzik."

"That will make things easier."

"Yes-zzik. We must talk. I need your help," said Zeke. "Come into my ship."

Ben was about to walk up the ramp when he remembered Andy had said that Zeke was a stranger. You don't go into a stranger's house even if they seem nice. That would probably also include a spaceship, even though nobody had ever told him whether or not he should go into a spaceship.

Suddenly, he thought of a safe way to talk to Zeke. He said, "I'd love to come in, Zeke, but I have to go to school soon. Why don't you come to school with me, then Andy and I can both help you? You can come in our car. Sue won't mind. We go in half an hour."

"Yes-zzik. What is…half an hour?"

Ben sighed. There was so much that Zeke didn't know.

"Ummmm," he said. "Go to the red car near the house and we will meet you soon."

"Yes-zzik." Zeke then pointed down to the ground near the ramp. "When Urssus-bul rose, there was an animal here. Hairy. Sharp teeth. Long tail. Is it safe to go out alone?"

Ben had images of a tiger or a wild animal. "Where?" he said, looking around alarmed.

"There it is-zzik," said Zeke, pointing to a spot at the base of a nearby tree. At first Ben saw nothing, but then noticed a leaf move, and a twitching tail.

"It's only a field mouse!" laughed Ben. "No need to be scared of them."

"Are they friends?" asked Zeke.

"No, this one is wild." Ben stepped towards the mouse, and it skipped away into the bush. "See?"

"Why do you grow mice if they do not like you?"

"We don't grow them. They're field mice. They live here. But my friend Lisa has some tame mice. They're friendly. Maybe she can show you one day."

"That would be acceptable," said Zeke.

"Great. I've got to go now. See you soon. Bye!"

Zeke watched Ben scramble out of the gully. Friendly and not friendly mice, he thought. How do animals know which others are friendly or not? Urssus3 is very strange. Nothing like Celesstis4.

Chapter 6

Miss Peters

Zeke was waiting next to the car when Ben and Sue came out of the house.

"Hi," said Sue. "Ben told me that you are going to our school. Want a lift?"

"Do I need to be higher?" asked Zeke.

Sue frowned. "I mean do you want to come to school with us?"

"Yes-zzik."

"By the way, Zeke," she said, "Ben may have told you that I'm a teacher at the school. Ben calls me 'Sue' at home, but you should call me 'Mrs Jones' like the other kids when we're at school. Okay?"

Zeke was confused. This is so very different from Celesstis4, he thought. Here they have different names for when they are in different places. How strange.

At school, Ben and Andy's teacher, Miss Peters, was very surprised to find that she had a new student. "Are you sure you're in my class?" she asked Zeke.

"I am not outside your class, therefore I must be in it," said Zeke.

The teacher smiled. "Very clever," she said. "Now, what's your name?"

"They call me Zzik."

"Zeke who?"

"Not Zzik Who, just Zzik," Zeke said.

"Miss Peters, ummmm, his name is Zeke…Martian," Andy said, thinking up a name quickly.

"But he's not really from Mars," Ben explained. "The Mars probes have proved that there is no life there at all."

This was getting too much for Miss Peters. "Thank you for that fascinating bit of information, Ben. Now all of you take a seat. I have to go and sort this mess out." She went next door to use the intercom to phone Mr Bell, the headmaster.

"Where do I take a seat to?" Zeke asked Andy.

"Just sit on one, don't take it anywhere."

But there was no desk or chair in the room for Zeke. After everyone sat down, Zeke went to the front of the room and sat on the teacher's chair.

"No!" Andy warned, but their teacher was already walking back through the door.

"We'd better find you a seat of your own, Zeke," Miss Peters said kindly. "I think you're a bit too young to stand in my shoes."

Zeke frowned. "I do not want to stand in your shoes. They are much too big for me. And they smell."

The class burst out laughing and Miss Peters' face turned bright red. Just then, Mr Bell walked in the room. He had heard everything. Andy groaned and put his head in his hands. Ben shrugged. It was true. Miss Peters did have big shoes. And they probably were smelly.

"Are you being cheeky, lad?" Mr Bell demanded.

Zeke froze. What was 'cheeky'? When he changed shape that morning, did he make his cheeks too big? He puffed them out and poked them with his fingers.

Everyone stared at him. What was this strange kid doing?

"I think I am fine," Zeke said finally. "I am not too cheeky."

Mr Bell coughed in surprise. "Listen kid," he said, "I don't know who you are, or why you've suddenly turned up in Miss Peters' class, but from now on you're going to be on your best behaviour. I don't want to hear another word out of you or I'll see you at the office!"

Zeke didn't know why Mr Bell was annoyed, or why the office sounded so scary, but he knew one thing for certain. He had to stay absolutely quiet for the rest of the day.

Chapter 7
The Surprise

At morning tea, Ben and Zeke sat in the eating area, in a corner far away from the other kids. Andy joined them. "You sure got in a lot of trouble this morning, Zeke," he said.

"That is correct-zzik," said Zeke.

Andy grinned at him. "Listen, Zeke, when kids agree with something they say 'yeah'. OK?"

"Yeah. OK?"

Andy shook his head. "No, not 'yeah OK', just 'yeah'."

"Just yeah."

"Yeah."

"Yeah. OK," said Zeke.

Andy frowned. Did Zeke really understand?

"Do all adults-zzik get as angry as your
teachers?" Zeke asked.

"Mr Bell is OK, and Miss Peters is not
usually that bad," said Andy. "You made her
cross."

"But I did nothing wrong. I did what I was
told!" said Zeke.

"When Miss Peters asked you to tell the
class where you came from, you didn't say
anything. Of course she got mad at you.
You're lucky she didn't send you to the
office," said Andy.

"But Mr Bell told me not to talk!" Zeke
cried. "I was doing what he told me to do. He
said, '*I don't want to hear another word out of you
or I'll see you at the office!*' So if I talk I get sent
to the office, and if I don't talk I could still
get sent to the office."

Ben nodded. "He did say that, but people
don't always say what they mean. I find them
hard to understand too. But that's because I
have Asperger's…"

"What's Asperger-zzik?" Zeke asked.

"Asperger Syndrome. It's called Asperger's for short. Kids with Asperger's find it hard to understand people and things they say and things they don't say."

"Are you an alien too?" Zeke asked.

"No, but sometimes I feel like one," said Ben.

"You are different from other humans?"

"You can say that again," Andy joked.

"You are different from other humans?" repeated Zeke.

Andy groaned. "I think I'm going crazy!"

The school bell rang for the end of morning tea. Saved by the bell, thought Andy.

"Zeke Martian!" The class watched Miss Peters get up from her desk and walk towards Zeke. Andy turned in his chair and said quietly to Zeke, "I think you should talk to her this time."

"Yeah?" Zeke said to the teacher.

"That's not how you answer a teacher," Miss Peters said gently.

Zeke didn't know what to say. Andy hissed, "Say 'yes', not 'yeah'."

"Yes," said Zeke, not knowing why. He was totally confused. Why did Andy tell him earlier to say 'yeah'?

"Yes, *what?*" prompted the teacher.

What did she want him to say? Zeke took a guess. "Yes, OK," he said.

A hush fell over the class. Miss Peters sighed. "Oh Zeke, I'm not sure where you come from, but you have a lot to learn. When you talk to me, please say 'Yes, Miss Peters' when I ask a question." She handed Zeke some papers. "I want you to take these forms home with you tonight and get your parents to fill them out over the weekend. And here are a school pad and pencil that you can use for today."

Zeke was puzzled by the paper and pencil. What was he supposed to do with them? School life was so confusing. Miss Peters walked back to her desk.

"Class," she said, "I have a surprise for you. This afternoon instead of your computer lessons we have some visitors from the Institute of Sport coming to teach us about team sports. It's a lovely day outside, so you can all put on your hats and run around in the sun and stretch your legs. Better than staring at computer screens. Won't that be fun? But now, it's time for science. We're going to need to clear the floor to do a few experiments. Please put away your things and move your desks and chairs to the sides of the room."

While the class was busily moving things around, Ben remained at his desk, stunned. He felt like crying and his throat was tight and sore. No computer lesson! How could Miss Peters do that to him? They only had one computer lesson a week and it was Ben's most favourite thing in all of school. Even when he was really sick, he came to school on computer day. And to make things worse, the lesson he hated most was sport!

"Come on, Ben," Andy called, but Ben didn't hear him. He clenched his fists and flapped them as tight little balls. No computer time! It was not fair! He clamped his teeth together to stop himself crying. He forgot about Zeke. He forgot his calming exercises that the support teacher had showed him. He forgot every rule he had been taught. And when Marnee, a quiet little girl who sat behind him, accidentally bumped his arm as she walked past, he forgot that she was small, gentle and kind. He lashed out and punched her hard, again and again and again.

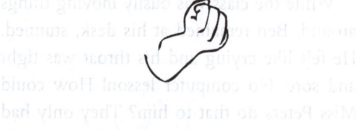

Chapter 8

Angry Anger

"**B**ut why did you hit her?" Sue asked, full of concern. "You're not a bully."

Sue and Ben sat with Mr Bell in his office. Mr Bell had asked Sue to talk to Ben, because he had refused to talk to anyone else.

"I didn't know I hit her," Ben sniffed.

"Come on, Ben," said Mr Bell, gruffly. "That's not good enough. The other kids say you hit her over and over again. You knew what you were doing."

"I didn't know..." His voice died away. How could he explain something that he didn't understand himself? He didn't remember hitting Marnee.

Sue put her arm around Ben. "Were you upset about something else?" she asked softly.

Ben started to cry. "Miss Peters told me that we'd have no computer time this week."

"This is about computer time?!?" Mr Bell cried in amazement. "Listen, son. If computer time means so much to you that you'd hit another kid just because it was cancelled, then I think I'll ban you from the computer room until the end of term. You're very lucky Marnee wasn't badly hurt, young man."

Ben felt sick. No computer time until the end of term! Life was so unfair!

"Ah, Mr Bell," said Sue, "I'm sure that's not necessary. Ben, let's work out what happened. Miss Peters told you that the computer lesson was cancelled, right?"

Ben nodded, sniffing. "And she said we'll have sport instead. I hate sport!"

"Ah, no computer, but extra sport. And that made you angry?"

Ben nodded.

"Marnee says she walked past and accidentally bumped you. Then you started hitting her. Do you remember any of that?"

"No," Ben said staring at the floor. "I like Marnee."

"Ben," Sue said, "You *did* hit her, and you hit her hard. You have to learn to recognize your own feelings and then deal with them without hurting others. What you felt was anger. Were your hands crunched up tight? Was your tummy sucked in hard? Were you biting your teeth?"

Ben nodded.

"That's anger, Ben, very angry anger. When you feel like that next time, try to get away by yourself for a while until the tightness goes. Remember what Miss Peters said? She wasn't punishing you. She thinks that going to sport is a treat. She was trying to be kind. Take the time to try to see things in a different way and then your anger won't be so bad."

"That's too hard," Ben said, his voice shaking with tears.

"I know it's hard, Ben, but it's worth it. Now it's time to say sorry to Marnee and if Mr Bell agrees, you need to go back to class."

Ben got up to leave, but stopped. "I don't want to," he said.

"It's important to apologize, Ben," Sue said.

"Not that. I'll apologize to Marnee. I mean I don't want to go back to class."

"You'll be fine, Ben," said Sue to his sad, sad face. "You can play on the computer when you get home. Have some time to yourself."

Chapter 9
The List

At lunchtime, Ben and Zeke sat alone in a corner of the eating area. Neither of them spoke. They both needed some quiet time where they didn't have to cope with other people's confusing ways. Ben opened his lunch case and scrunched his nose up in disgust. Cheese sandwiches! He always had peanut butter sandwiches for lunch. *Always.*

Except once before. That time they had run out of peanut butter at home. They must have run out again. He left his sandwiches in the case and took out the banana. Then he closed the case and put it away in his bag. It didn't occur to him to give his sandwiches to Zeke.

But Zeke wasn't hungry. He'd filled up on travel rations that morning... Deltar seed pods, his favourite.

At the end of lunchtime, Andy came over to chat to Ben and Zeke. All the other kids had gone to play sport or run around with their friends.

"I'm having a bad day," said Ben.

"Me too," said Zeke.

"That's life," said Andy. "Actually, I think it's been a pretty good day. Those science experiments were fun and we still have sport this afternoon. I hope we play basketball. Then it'll be a great day."

"I wish I was home," said Zeke.

"That's right!" Ben exclaimed. "You said you needed help to get home. Remember, Andy, I told you about that this morning."

"Yeah," cried Andy, suddenly remembering too. "Tell us what we can do. I'm dying to know how we could possibly help an alien."

"No-zzik. That would be too much. You need not die to help me," said Zeke.

Andy laughed. "That's something Ben would say."

Zeke took a piece of paper from his pocket. "All I want are some things before I can leave your planet. I wrote them down in your words. I need these before I leave tomorrow."

Ben took the paper and read:

Information storage device

Energy source

Sustenance

Clothing

"I must have these things-zzik. The starship departs from Urssus5 tomorrow night and I cannot leave Urssus3 without them."

"What starship?" Ben cried, jumping to his feet, flapping his hands. This was exciting!

"I am with a survey mission exploring this area of space. Our starship is stationed on the dark side of Urssus5."

"Can someone explain to me what this Urssus is all about?" asked Andy.

"Urssus is his name for the planets in our solar system," explained Ben. He counted off the planets from the sun on his fingers.

"So you have to get to Jupiter by tomorrow night or you're trapped here forever, right?" he asked Zeke.

"Not exactly…"

But Ben was too excited to listen. "Let's go through the list again."

Andy held the list, puzzled. "What's an 'information storage device'?"

"That's easy," said Ben. "A CD-ROM or a video cassette or something like that."

"What about 'sustenance'?" asked Andy.

"Food," said Ben. "We have these things at home. Is this all you need, Zeke?"

"Yes. Yeah. OK. Right," said Zeke.

Chapter 10
Lisa

There were two lessons on Friday afternoon. Art and computer class. But today, instead of computer class, there was going to be sport. After art, Ben trudged along with Andy and Zeke and the rest of his class to the oval. There were kids everywhere. Half the school must be there. Miss Peters should have said that other classes were coming too. He wasn't ready for this. All those kids. All the noise!

"Ben!"

He heard Lisa's squeaky voice call his name, but couldn't see where she was in the crowd. Lisa Flint was Ben's friend from the Asperger Support Group. She was the friend who liked mice, the friend he had told Zeke about. Ben had only known her for a couple of months, but as soon as they had met they got on really well. She was in the grade above him, and was the only other Asperger kid in the school. Some kids teased Ben for liking a girl, but he didn't care.

"Ben, over yonder!"

Then Ben saw Lisa walking towards him.

"I hate it out here," said Lisa as soon as she caught up with them. "People everywhere." Lisa's fair hair was plaited into coils on each side of her head. They looked like little ears. Mouse ears.

"I also hate it here. Too many things are happening," said Zeke.

Lisa smiled at him. She didn't know him, but this was one kid she understood. "I brought Paddy to school," she said. She opened the top of her pocket, and her pet mouse shuffled its head out and wiggled its nose in the air.

"Lisa!" Andy gasped. "The teachers will kill you if they see that!"

"Poor children of Urssus3," said Zeke. "How terrible it must be to die for taking animals-zzik to school."

"They won't *really* kill her," Andy explained, "but she could get into heaps of trouble."

"The mummy mouse had seven babies last night," said Lisa. "They're all tiny pinky blobs. Mum thinks they're ugly, but I love them. I called them Karlos, Bekky, Sashy and Sam, and Tahlsey and Sharnsy and Spooky. Spooky is the smallest one. We had to put Paddy into another cage in case he eats them. He's the daddy. Get it, Paddy Daddy?"

Ben laughed. "That sounds cute."

Andy frowned. He didn't see what was funny.

"I had to bring Paddy to school. He'd be lonely at home all by himself. Wouldn't you, my wee, sleekit, cow'rin, tim'rous beastie."

She tickled her mouse behind its ears, then slipped it back into her pocket.

"Wee what?" asked Ben.

"Wee, sleekit, cow'rin, tim'rous beastie. It means my scared little critter. It's from a poem by Robert Burns."

Andy shuffled his feet. "No offence but I don't really want to listen to Lisa talking forever about mice and poetry or whatever else she's into today. It's boring. I'm going to see if they're teaching basketball, and throw a few hoops or something. See ya later."

He jogged away.

Ben didn't mind. He knew Andy loved his sport.

"I saw a mouse-zzik this morning," said Zeke. "It was not friendly. Can I hold this one? Is it safe?"

Lisa stared at Zeke. "You talk funny. Who are you?"

"This is Zeke," said Ben. "He's from outer space. His spaceship crashed in the gully at my place. It's shiny and round with flashing lights."

"Unreal!" said Lisa. "That makes you an alien. My mousies would love to have a ride on your ship. Wouldn't you, Paddy?" She coaxed the mouse from her pocket and handed it over to Zeke, who held it by the tail to keep his fingers away from its teeth.

"Not by the tail!" Lisa squeaked, cupping Zeke's fingers under the mouse's body. "Hold mice nice."

"We do not have creatures this tame where I come from," Zeke explained. "I have never held an animal so small."

"Poor you. Where are you from anyway?"

Zeke looked around the sky, squinted, and pointed. "About there," he said.

"How romantic," Lisa sighed. "Out in the stars," and in her sweetest voice she began:

> *Far from the fiery noon, and eve's one star,*
> *Sat gray-hair'd Saturn, quiet as a stone.*

"What was that?" asked Ben.

"It's from a poem by Keats. It's sooo romantic."

"What's Keats?"

"He was a poet and he wrote plays. About 200 years ago."

"I don't think a dead man's poems are that romantic," Ben said. He counted the planets on his fingers. "Anyway, he got it wrong. It's not Saturn. It's Urssus6."

"That's not very romantic," sniffed Lisa.

"Hey," said Ben, pointing. "Look at the rubbish area."

In the middle of the junk heap was a large cardboard refrigerator box splattered with paint and glue. It had obviously been used in art class. Lisa nodded, understanding what Ben was thinking. "Lead on, McDuff," she whispered. Ben and Zeke looked around. Who was McDuff? Probably more poetry.

Together they crept to the box and dragged it behind some bushes. "Once more into the breach, dear friends," said Lisa as the three of them crawled inside the opening.

Away from the oval, away from the noise, away from sport, and away from crowd, Lisa, Ben and Zeke huddled at the back of the box

and talked about computers and space,
poetry and mice.

Chapter 11

Leaving For Good

"Sue, can Zeke come over this afternoon?" Ben asked as he and Zeke got in the car after school finished.

"Sure. Only if that's all right with your parents, Zeke. I'll have to meet them one day."

"That will not be possible, Mrs Sue Jones. I am leaving tomorrow," Zeke said.

"Leaving? For good?"

"Yes, yeah, OK, Mrs Sue Jones. It will not be bad."

"Oh, what a shame. It is nice for Ben to have a friend next door."

71

What door was she was talking about, thought Zeke. He stayed quiet all the way home.

When they got home Ben and Zeke had a slice of cake. While they were eating, Grandma came in with a large bundle of paper.

"How's the assignment going, Ma?" Sue asked, making her a cup of tea.

"Very well, thank you. A bit slowly though. I took a bit of time off and did some more baking today. But I am enjoying using my brain again." She turned to Ben. "I'm awfully sorry, Ben, but I haven't found any evidence of life on other planets yet."

Ben looked at her blankly. "But Zeke's an alien, and he's right here," he said.

Grandma laughed. "Of course he is. We just haven't found his planet yet."

"That's right," Zeke agreed. "You humans are very unsophisticated when it comes to interplanetary mobility. However I extrapolate-zzik that once you discover light-drive it will take little more than five Urssus3 years to discover the Celesstis System and our small colony of Huubble Snitz that live there."

"Oh," Grandma managed to say.

"Then how about you kids go Huubble Snitz hunting while I get dinner ready," Sue laughed.

When they were outside, Ben said, "Let's start getting the things you need to fix your spaceship."

"Zzik, you do not comprehend my need. I don't...," Zeke began.

But Ben wasn't listening. "The first thing that you had on your list was an information storage device. What about a video cassette? Will that do?"

"Yes-zzik."

"Can you use them in your ship? Did your information device get damaged when you crashed?" Ben asked, as they started walking back to the house.

"That is not...," Zeke said, but as the clothes line came into view Ben interrupted.

"You need clothing too, right? Why not take something from here. What about one of Dad's work shirts?"

"Yes-zzik," Zeke said, as he watched Ben take a shirt from an assortment of items flapping in the breeze.

Ben then ran inside and was soon back with a video cassette. It was an old one he found at the back of the cupboard on which Sue had taped *Gone with the Wind.* It was probably a science show and he didn't think she'd miss it.

"What else do you need?" he asked. "Food."

"I don't..." Zeke began.

"I know!" Ben cried, cutting him off again. "Grandma has a cake cooling down inside. You love cake, Zeke."

Soon he was back with a cake tin.

"And the last one is an energy source. That sounds important," said Ben. He thought for a moment. "I know. There are batteries in the TV, and you still have it in your ship. I can leave them with you. Are they good enough for the energy source you need?"

"Yes-zzik," said Zeke. "They meet my needs."

Ben helped Zeke take the batteries, cake, video tape and work shirt to the spaceship, then returned home with the TV.

Well done, he thought. He felt proud. It wasn't every day that he got to help an alien stranded on Earth.

leave them with you. Are they good enough for the energy source you need?"

"Yes-zxik," said Zeke. "They meet my needs."

Ben helped Zeke take the batteries, cake, video tape and work shirt to the spaceship, then returned home with the TV.

Well done, he thought. He felt proud. It wasn't every day that he got to help an alien stranded on Earth.

Chapter 12
But Dad!

Whehn Dad came home that night, Ben challenged him to a game of chess.

"Want to beat me again?" Dad laughed. "I don't know why I bother playing with you. You always win."

"You won once, Dad," said Ben as he set up the pieces.

"Once in five years is not a good record."

"I'll help you, Jack," said Sue as she came up behind him, putting her arm around his shoulders. "Two heads are better than one."

Dad turned and hugged her close. "And with a head as pretty as yours, we're sure to win this time." He kissed her gently on the forehead.

"No kissing, you two!" Ben cried. "And no mushy stuff. Chess is a serious game."

"Let's get serious then," Sue chuckled. "Can we be white?"

"OK," Ben agreed.

They were well into the game when Grandma came into the room. "Who's winning?" she asked.

"Ben!" said Sue and Dad together, then giggled.

"They're not trying hard, Grandma," Ben said. "They keep fooling around. Can't you make them behave?"

"I gave up on Jack years ago," Grandma laughed. "And Sue's a bit old for me to order around."

Ben glanced from Grandma, to Sue, to Dad. It was nice having a new mum. Sue made the group into a family.

"By the way," Grandma added, "has any one see a cake floating around? I made three, but one's missing."

"Cakes don't float, Grandma. Besides I gave it to Zeke," Ben said.

"You what?" Dad said. The tone in the room changed quickly, but Ben didn't notice.

"I gave the cake to Zeke," Ben repeated. "He wanted it. Your move, Dad."

Dad pushed the board to one side. Ben, thinking Dad was still in a playful mood, said, "Come on, Dad. It's your move."

"Let's forget the game for a minute," Dad said seriously, making Ben nervous. He sensed he was in trouble, but wasn't sure why yet.

"I've got to get this right," said Dad. "Zeke asked for the cake. So you gave it to him. And you didn't ask Grandma?"

Ben nodded.

"Did you give Zeke anything else?"

"Yes. Some batteries, a video tape, and one of your work shirts. Zeke said he needed them."

"My work shirt!" said Dad.

"What video?" asked Sue.

"The science one. *Gone with the Wind.*"

"Oh, Ben," Sue sighed. "That was my favourite."

Dad shook his head. "And because he asked, you gave all these things to him?"

Ben nodded.

Dad stiffened. "I don't believe this, Ben. Why would you give a complete stranger all those things? What were you thinking?"

"Zeke's not a stranger. He's my friend."

"Someone you've known for one day is still a stranger, Ben. Why did you give him those things?"

"He wanted them!"

"Grandma wanted her cake too. And I want my shirt. Did you think of that?"

"No."

Dad stood up, bumping the board. The black queen fell on its side. Ben leaned across and set her upright.

"Ben," Dad said, with teeth clenched. "Right now I feel very angry with you. Sometimes I can't understand the things you do. I'm going outside for a while so I can think straight, and we'll talk later when I calm down. Go to your room until then." He pointed towards the door.

"But Dad…!" Ben cried.

"Go!"

"But Dad…!"

"Go!" Dad yelled louder.

"But Dad…!" Ben bawled, his face screwed up in confusion.

Dad turned and walked out of the room.

Sue said to Grandma, "You stay with Ben, I'll go to Jack," and she slipped out the door.

Dad stood up, bumping the board. The black queen fell on its side. Ben leaned across and set her upright.

"Ben," Dad said, with teeth clenched. "Right now I feel very angry with you. Sometimes I can't understand the things you do. I'm going outside for a while so I can think straight, and we'll talk later when I calm down. Go to your room until then." He pointed towards the door.

"But Dad..." Ben cried.

"Go!"

"But Dad..."

"Go!" Dad yelled louder.

"But Dad..." Ben bawled, his face screwed up in confusion.

Dad turned and walked out of the room. Sue said to Grandma, "You stay with Ben, I'll go to Jack," and she slipped out the door.

Chapter 13

Zeke's Trick

Grandma led Ben back to his room where he curled up on the bed sobbing.

"Ben, I know you're upset and right now you don't understand why your dad is mad at you, but try to think of how we all feel that you gave our things away. Can you do that?"

Ben wept louder and Grandma wasn't sure he heard her. She left the room sadly, knowing that when he was as upset as this, he needed time to himself to calm down. Poor Ben. He found it hard to see how his actions affected other people. But he was clever and she knew that once he'd talked things through, Ben would realize his mistakes.

On the veranda, Dad paced backwards and forwards. Sue sat on the edge of a wicker chair.

"Why did he do it?" Dad said in frustration. "It's so wrong to give away things he doesn't own. Can't he see that?"

"I don't think he does," Sue sighed. "He's a sweet, trusting kid, that's all. He probably thought he was being helpful."

"But who was he helping? Certainly not us. Who is this Zeke anyway? And why would some kid want my work shirt? Nothing makes sense."

Inside, Ben's sobbing slowed to jerky sniffs. Dad's words carried in the evening air, and Ben heard them through the window. Suddenly Ben felt a pang of worry. Why *would* Zeke need a cake and an old shirt and the other things? None of them could help repair a spaceship. Had Zeke tricked him?

The bedroom door opened and Sue and Dad came in. Confused and upset, Ben stared at the floor. He hated being in trouble, especially when he didn't really know what he'd done wrong. Dad sat on the chair and Sue sat next to Ben on the bed. She said gently, "Ben, we need to talk about what you did today. It was wrong to give Zeke all those things. Why did you do it?"

"He needed them!" Ben whimpered, but at the back of his mind he thought, what for?

"We need those things too, Ben," Sue pointed out. "You gave Zeke things that were not yours to give. Did you think about how we would feel when we found our things gone?"

Ben shook his head.

Dad took a notepad and pen from a shelf and leaned close.

"Think of it this way." He drew a stick figure of Grandma. In a bubble above her head he wrote, "I spent hours baking a cake and now it has gone!"

"Here's Grandma. How do you think she feels when she loses her cake?"

"Sad, but Zeke…"

"Forget Zeke for a while. Think about how your actions affect others."

Dad then drew a stick figure of himself. Above it he wrote, "I am sad. My shirt is gone." Then above a picture of Sue he drew a sad face.

"See how many people are sad because of what you did."

"But Zeke…"

"I don't care about Zeke. I care about you. You must think for yourself. You can't let one kid you just met change every rule you know to be right. See how many people are sad all because you made Zeke happy. It's not right, Ben."

Ben nodded, starting to understand.

Sue added, "How would you feel if we gave your computer away to a man we just met because he said he wanted one?"

"Bad."

"Exactly. It would be wrong for us to do that. You can't trust strangers, Ben. And even if people you meet seem nice and friendly, you mustn't do what they ask without thinking first."

Ben nodded. Now things were beginning to make sense.

"I love you, Ben," Dad said, "And so do Sue and Grandma, but we can't be with you all the time. You have to learn to make right decisions on your own. I know that having Asperger's means you don't always understand rules that well, especially if you haven't been told the rules clearly, but you still have a wonderful brain. You can learn to think and decide if things are right or wrong all by yourself."

"OK, Dad," Ben said. "I'll try." Sue hugged him. "You're a good kid, Ben. You know we want the best for you, that's why we get upset when you do something silly and dangerous."

"I know. I'm sorry."

"You'll have to get all the things back, Ben, and don't tell me Zeke needs them," Dad said as Ben opened his mouth to speak. "He can't have them."

"OK," Ben said in a small voice.

When Sue and Dad had gone, Ben stood at the window and watched the sun set through orange red clouds. Life was hard. People were confusing. Rules changed too often. This morning Zeke was his friend. Now Zeke was a stranger and not to be trusted. How could he get everything back and make everyone else happy again? He couldn't go to the spaceship tonight. It was too late and besides, it might be dangerous to go alone. Tomorrow. He could go tomorrow with Andy. Tomorrow he would make things right again.

Chapter 14

The Notes

Andy arrived early on Saturday morning. They went into Ben's room.

"I'm in trouble. I don't know how to get them back," Ben said, as soon as he'd shut the door.

"Whoooah. Slow down," Andy said. "What do you have to get back?"

"I gave Zeke Sue's video, Dad's shirt, Grandma's cake, and some batteries. The things he had on his list. Dad said he wants them back."

"You gave Zeke all those things? You're crazy."

"I know. Now. But I've been thinking. Why would Zeke need those things anyway? They can't help him fly a ship."

"I've been thinking the same thing," Andy agreed. "It's fair enough that he'd want one of your grandma's cakes. They're delicious. But why did he want your dad's shirt? It won't fix a ship. And when we saw him first, he had four legs and wasn't wearing a shirt anyway. And what about the video? And the batteries? Do you think they'd work in his ship?"

It was becoming clearer to Ben now. They'd been tricked! Zeke was an alien and they shouldn't have trusted him. He turned to Andy. "What do we do now? I've got to get those things back. I was going to go by myself last night, but then I thought it'd be safer if we went together. He's leaving today."

"Maybe we should get your dad to come with us. Does he know that Zeke's an alien?"

"I'm not sure." Ben thought back. "We told Sue and Grandma. But they weren't worried."

"I don't think they believed us," said Andy, "or they would have freaked out. We've got to find your dad. He will know what to do."

Andy and Ben looked around the house. Sue was in the study. Grandma was probably in her flat. Dad was nowhere to be seen.

"Maybe he's doing the mowing," said Ben. "He does that on Saturdays. If he does he'll see Zeke's spaceship for sure."

They ran outside. Where was Dad? He wasn't near the pool. He wasn't on the mower. He wasn't anywhere. "Where can he be?" Ben cried, starting to panic. They went to the start of the track, to see if Dad was anywhere down near the spaceship. Carefully, they peered into the gully. They saw broken branches, but no spaceship. The spaceship was gone!

Oh no! they thought. Zeke's got Dad!

"Hello boys."

Ben and Andy turned around in alarm. Dad!

"What's up? You look like you've seen a ghost. Listen, I'm going to mow out here soon. Make sure you keep out of the way." He headed back to the shed.

"At least your dad's safe," said Andy in relief. "But if Zeke's gone, we can't get your stuff back."

"What's that?" asked Ben, pointing at a silvery shape in the gully.

"Don't know. I don't like the look of it though," said Andy. "Could be dangerous."

"Let's check it out...carefully," Ben added, seeing the nervousness on Andy's face.

The two boys crept down into the gully, hiding behind trees and rocks as they went.

"It's some sort of box," Ben said finally, peering around a shrub.

"Look through the slats!" Andy said. "I think all your stuff's inside!"

"You're right!" Ben exclaimed. They ran to the crate and opened it. Everything Ben had given to Zeke was inside.

"What's that?" said Andy, pointing to a piece of paper at the bottom of the box.

"It's a note," said Ben. He picked it up and read it aloud...

My alien friend Ben,

I heard your dad and Mrs Sue Jones talking outside your house last night. They were angry with you for giving me things. It is my fault. I asked you to help me. So I am going now and will cause no more trouble.

I do not need the things to fix my ship. My ship is not damaged. The scratches and broken lights were from an asteroid in the Ornicle System.

I tried to explain but you did not want to know. I needed the things for an assignment. When we survey a solar system like Urssus, we each visit a planet and collect the items set for us. The one who collects the most items wins an award. That is why I didn't want to leave Urssus3 without the things on the list.

I am giving back your items in this space crate. They are more important to you. But I need the space crate back. I will orbit Urssus3 before leaving for Urssus5. Please leave the crate exactly where you found it, and I will beam it back to my ship when I pass over here again at 10 o'clock this morning in your time.

Farewell. Zzik

"So that's what it was all about," said Ben. "An assignment, and now he'll fail because of us."

They were silent for a while, thinking of Zeke and all that had happened.

Suddenly Andy said, "I just had a thought. What's the time?"

Ben looked at his watch. "9.31 a.m. and 20 seconds. And if I'm thinking what you're thinking, we don't have much time!"

Chapter 15

I Am So Happy,
I Could Zzborgle

"**W**hat's the time now?" asked Andy, as they put the crate back down exactly where they had found it.

"9.57 a.m. and ten seconds," said Ben, as he wiped his brow. "Just in time."

It had been a very busy half hour. Running around the house, they had collected all the things that Zeke needed to win his award. Things that wouldn't get Ben into trouble. A piece of clothing; one of Ben's ragged old shirts that didn't fit him anymore. An energy source, an old battery that no longer worked. Sustenance, the cheese sandwich from Ben's school lunch case. The information storage device was a kid's song tape that Ben had from when he was young.

Andy picked it up and teased, "*Toot Toot the Train Tunes*! Are you sure you won't miss this? I bet you listen to it every night."

"I do not! But I used to love trains when I was little."

"I remember. That's all you talked about in Grade 1."

"Put it back. Zeke's going to beam it up in two minutes."

"Have you got the note ready?" Andy asked.

"Yep," Ben said, and read...

To Zeke,

Here are the four things you wanted. They aren't important to us so we won't get into trouble this time.

Good luck on your assignment.

From your friends, Ben and Andy

"Sounds good," Andy said, putting it in the crate and closing the lid. They climbed to the track on top of the gully and sat down, and watched, and waited.

They did not see the field mouse as it scurried through the leaves on the gully floor. "Cheese!" it thought in its little brain, as it sniffed and scampered through the silver slats. And then, in a flash, the space crate disappeared.

For some minutes Ben and Andy stayed seated on the track. The most exciting time in their lives was now over. How quickly everything had happened. Then out of the corners of their eyes they saw another flash on the gully floor. They ran down and picked up two pieces of paper. The first read:

Ben and Andy,

Thank you. I am so happy I could zzborgle.

I have nothing here to give you in return. Except one thing, which I have written on

> the back of this paper. You won't under-
> stand any of this yet, but with Ben's
> clever brain and love of maths, one day
> you may be able to work out what it
> says. If you do, you will see that the
> last line is made up of the co-ordinates
> for my planet Celesstis4, in a galaxy
> far, far from Urssus3. Perhaps in the
> future you will come to visit me.
> Your very best friend, Zzik

"Wow!" cried Ben. "This is the most important thing in the whole wide world!"

"It's amazing!" said Andy. "What's on the second note?"

> Thank you too for the mouse. I will re-
> member you always.
> Zzik

"Mouse? What mouse!??" cried Ben

Epilogue

Three Urssus3 rotations later, ⊇⋊⥾⊇ stood on all four suckers in front of the Grand Master of Starship Surveyor10148. Behind him stood the crew and their younglings. The Grand Master rotated his eyes around the audience and hooted in his loudest Huubble-speak, "And the highest award goes to ⊇⋊⥾⊇ whom the aliens of Urssus3 called…Zzik."

The gathering of Huubble Snitz honked and stomped their suckers on the floor with squishy splook-splosh sounds.

The Grand Master waited for silence, then continued. "Not only did ⊇⋊⥾⊇ collect every single item on his list, but no other mission found any of the items on any other planet in orbit of Urssus-bul."

The crowd went wild! They lifted ƨ✕Ϛƨ into the air, honking, bellowing and screeching in delight.

ƨ✕Ϛƨ was given a Celesstis-year's worth of extra food vouchers and all four of his suckers were pressed onto the starship's Wall of Excellence.

Much, much later, after the celebrations were over, the starship dimmed its lights for a rest period. The younglings withdrew their eyes back into their heads, and with their learning probes in place they went to sleep for that night's lessons. ƨ✕Ϛƨ slid from his sleeping couch and pulled a small eco-crate from his cupboard. His eyes stretched out to see the field mouse and her five new pink blobby babies, and he dropped in some more fresh water and Blaxxion grainseed. This was one thing from Urssus3 that he had not told the Grand Master about. What a great gift from Ben and Andy, he thought.

Little did know, but this was just the beginning of what was to become the great mouse plague of the starships of Celesstis. But that's another story.

★★★★★★★

Useful addresses

If you want to find out more about Asperger Syndrome, these organisations are a good place to start:

Autism Association Queensland Inc.
The Executive Director
PO Box 363,
Sunnybank QLD 4109
Australia
Email: mailbox@autismqld.asn.au
Tel: 617 3273 0000

Asperger's Syndrome Support Network (Queensland) Inc.
PO Box 123
Lawnton QLD 4501
Australia
Email: revans@powerup.com.au
Tel: 617 3285 7001

The National Autistic Society
393 City Road
London EC1V 1NE
Tel: 020 7833 2299

Autism Society of America Inc.
7910 Woodmont Avenue, Suite 650
Bethesda
MD 20814–3015
USA
Tel: 301 657 0881

Autism Society of Canada

129 Yorkville Avenue, Suite 202
Toronto
Ontario M5R 1C4
Canada
Tel: 416 922 0302

The ASPEN (Asperger Syndrome Education Network) Society of America Inc.

PO Box 2577
Jacksonville
FL 32203–2577
USA
Tel: 904 745 6741

Asperger's Syndrome Support Network

c/o VACCA
PO Box 235
Ashburton
Victoria 3147
Australia

Autistic Association of New Zealand

PO Box 7305
Sydenham
Christchurch
New Zealand
Tel: 03 332 1038

Websites

National Autistic Society

http://www.oneworld.org/autism_uk/index.html

OASIS (Online Asperger Syndrome Information and Support)

http://www.udel.edu/bkirby/asperger/

The Centre for the Study of Autism

http://www.autism.org

Asperger's Disorder Homepage

http://www.aspergers.com

Blue Bottle Mystery

An Asperger Adventure

Kathy Hoopman

Nothing is quite the same after Ben and his friend Andy find an old bottle in the school yard. What is the strange wisp of smoke that keeps following them around? What mysterious forces have been unleashed? Things become even more complicated when Ben is diagnosed with Asperger Syndrome.

Blue Bottle Mystery is great fun to read and will keep you guessing until the end.

'I read this book in under an hour and then immediately picked it up and read it again, much to my brother's disappointment ("It's my book!")... It was a wonderful to listen to his cries of "Oh now I understand," "I do that," "Aspergers – that's what I have." We shall have to buy another copy because both my brother and I love it too much to let the other have a read... Congratulations on a truly wonderful book.'

– *Clare Truman (age 14)*

Kathy Hoopmann is a primary school teacher and children's author who lives near Brisbane in Queensland, Australia. She enjoys camping, walking on the beach, and writing on the computer for hours on end. She is married with three children, two zebra finches, a cat and dozens of wild birds that feed on her back deck. Kathy has been involved with children with Asperger syndrome for many years.

ISBN 978 1 85302 978 3

Lisa and the Lacemaker

An Asperger Adventure

Kathy Hoopmann

When Lisa discovers a derelict hut in her friend Ben's backyard, she delights in exploring the remnants of an era long gone. Imagine her surprisewhen Great Aunt Hannah moves into a nursing home nearby, and reveals that once she was a servant in those very rooms. The old lady draws Lisa into the art of lace making and through the criss-crossing of threads, Lisa is helped to understand her own Asperger Syndrome. But Great Aunt Hannah also has a secret and now it is up to Lisa to confront the mysterious Lacemaker and put the past to rest.

'Kathy Hoopmann has written a captivating adventure story but has also created a unique and accurate insight into the experiences and inner thoughts of a girl with Asperger's syndrome. Her central character faces challenges and develops coping strategies that we have only recently recognized. Children, parents and teachers will find the story both entertaining and an opportunity for education.'

– Tony Attwood

ISBN 978 1 84310 071 3